INTO THE GRAVE

Laura Shenton

INTO THE GRAVE

Laura Shenton

Iridescent Toad Publishing

Iridescent Toad Publishing.

Cover by SG Designs.

First edition. ISBN: 978-1-913779-94-8

They say there's a place
Between life and death
It's not quite Heaven
It's not quite Hell
But it's a place of existence
Nevertheless

Within it dwells
A yearning
A frantic desperation
For peace at last
But will it come?

Chapter One

James squinted through the blazing sunrays that shone down on his weary face. As his old car rattled along the dusty road, his throat ached for the relief of a cold drink. Rolling down the window in frustration, he welcomed the refreshing gust of air that rushed into the stuffy vehicle.

The calming sounds of nature coming from the nearby woods only served to make him more aware of how truly isolated he was from suburbia. His head ached from the heavy atmosphere in the air – a telltale sign that a storm was coming. It would surely clear the humidity eventually, but still, the thought was just as daunting as the endless, winding road ahead. There were no streetlights to guide him and no other cars in sight. By nightfall, he would have to drive even more cautiously, his headlights the only illumination to depend on.

A forceful wind whirled through the treetops, causing enough of a stir for James to notice the faint outline of a house in the distance. Its tall chimney, bent at an angle, stood out against the sky.

He edged his car along the country road until he noticed a stony path up ahead. Although it wasn't wide, it was still accessible. He reasoned that if he followed it into the woods, it would probably lead to the house that he'd seen behind the trees. He wasn't sure however, that it would be the best option.

Still with a choice of routes forking out before him, he drove slowly, ever-mindful of the upcoming potholes and bumps. As rain began to pelt the roof of his car, he hoped desperately that a kind stranger would be willing to offer him shelter for the night. He prayed for a single soul out there who would take him in, no matter how meagre his coin. His mind raced at the thought of what would become of him if he was left alone to face the cruel, unforgiving elements.

He decided to risk it; with a flick of his wrist, he directed the car towards the woods. Thankfully, his wheels held steady against the varied terrain, and soon enough, the large house loomed into view. It was surrounded by iron bars too high for anyone to scale. At the top of them were several beautifully-carved stone gargoyles. The yard beyond the bars was filled with weeds and unkempt plants.

Despite the hollow silence and a pervading sense of dread that settled deep within his bones, James held his breath as he pulled the key out of the ignition, concerned that his ancient car wouldn't start up again. It was always a worry to him. Glancing at his reflection in the side mirror, he could see the signs of his exhaustion. His eyes were sunken and surrounded by dark circles, but he still looked neat and presentable overall.

He got out of his car and nervously glanced around, checking to ensure that his only abode was safe in its makeshift parking spot under a large, looming oak tree. He then walked towards the gate. Up close, he noticed that the tall iron bars were rusty and chipped. Feeling their sharp edges against his skin, he pushed on them forcefully. With a loud creak and a groan of metal, heavy and unforgiving, they finally gave way.

As he approached the house, he noticed the true

enormity of the imposing structure – it was more like a mansion. The walls were covered in ivy, the hardy plant starkly contrasting with the worn paintwork, which extended onto the balcony and pillars.

It was getting dark, but with the bright moonlight, James still managed to get a good look at his surroundings. The garden was a mess, but the lavender bushes were in full bloom. As he stared at their vibrant colours and took in their powdery scent, a painful pang of regret surged through his entire being. He used to give the same flowers as a gift to his beloved girlfriend, before she had left him. He should have seen it coming; she wanted a life of riches, but he had been out of work for far too long. The thought stung him like a thousand knives, driving him forward until his fingertips brushed against one of the velvety lavender stems.

Instinctively feeling the need to look around, James noticed a woman at the far end of the garden. Silhouetted by the darkening sky, her frame was slender. The stream of her pale blue dress billowed around her in the breeze. The abundance of elegant fabric made it seem as though she was floating rather than walking. Her veil flowed all the way down to her feet, dancing harmoniously with her.

The woman was clearly searching for something, or someone. She moved gracefully towards James, almost as if her feet were not in contact with the ground. Before he could get her attention though, she diverted towards the house, and quickly vanished.

Keen to talk to his potential host, James walked closer towards the house, taking in the neglected garden. There were weeds poking out of the cracks in the walkway. The entire place seemed as though it had been left to the mercies of time.

This place is clearly in need of some work. Perhaps there could be a chance of a job in it for me.

Carefully stepping onto the porch, James noted how the wood beneath his feet groaned in protest. It didn't seem secure or dependable. He seized the chance to gaze through one of the house's many windows. Despite the dusty layer, he could lean in closely enough to see. A single candle on a single stump burned in the corner of the room. It cast a faint, wavering light that danced in the darkness.

Nervously, he stood up straight and rolled back his shoulders as he turned his attention to the menacing gargoyle brass knocker on the front door. He pounded it against the decaying wood with fierce determination.

He was greeted by only stillness and silence.

Once again he pounded the brass knocker against the door.

"Hello?" he called out.

Met with no response, he let out a frustrated sigh.

Unwilling to accept defeat, James tested the door handle. He was surprised to find that although it was weighty, the door wasn't locked.

As his foot dared to breach the sacred threshold of the house, an ominous shiver crawled up his spine. In an instant, a raven, its ebony wings slicing through the air like a sinister omen, shattered the silence, jolting James to the very core. Cawing assertively, the threatening bird perched on a ledge and stared at James from within the shadows, its form almost hidden by the darkness, but revealed by its piercing eyes.

With wings as dark as charcoal, it seemed poised to defend its territory.

The raven then shifted on its feet. Suddenly, it flew into the air, screeching an unintelligible warning before landing elsewhere in the room. James held his breath, daunted by the bird's presence.

I refuse to be intimidated by a mere bird.

His heart raced as he cautiously took a few more steps inside the house. He was hesitant to let the door close behind him, almost as if doing so would make him a prisoner.

Gathering his resolve, he pushed himself to continue moving forward, despite the rising tension that hung in the air.

"Is there anybody here?" he called out into the darkness.

His voice echoed around, only to be met with complete silence.

Not only did the house smell musty, but everything within it was tainted with age. The furnishings ranged from worn-out to completely defunct, clearly having been residents of the house for longer than anyone could remember.

Further ahead, James spotted an open door that led into a room, revealing a painting illuminated solely by a sliver of moonlight streaming in from a nearby window. The woman in the painting was dressed in tattered clothing and bore an air of exhaustion in her posture. Strangely, the smile on her face held an unsettling, almost unnatural, sense of sinister mirth. Although she appeared to be no older than her early thirties, she seemed frail, vulnerable and tired. The sadness in her eyes looked as though she was apologising for her very presence.

Despite the enormous jagged crack running through the centre of the glass that covered the painting, James could still make out the details. It appeared as though a sharp, pointed object had been used to strike the portrait viciously – perhaps with multiple jabbing motions having been applied several times over.

As he bent forward to peer closer at the painting, he noticed a name etched into the brass at the bottom of the frame. His brow furrowed as he read it out loud.

"Iris Dalton."

He couldn't help but be taken in by the painting. The woman's energy seemed to take over the entire room.

James sensed that he had already ventured too far to turn back. His gaze turned to the candle at the far side of the room. A source of light, and a comforting anchor amidst the darkness that surrounded him, it flickered softly.

He was surprised to notice that, despite how unforgiving the heat of the day had been, a roaring fire danced on the hearth. Not far from the fireplace was a wooden table. Upon it was a fruit bowl that brimmed with ripe grapes and rosy apples. Moreover, there was some type of pâté that seemed to have been tasted recently; it did not seem as though it had expired.

Noticing a single set of cutlery that must have been carelessly thrown down in a clatter of urgency, James stood aghast. He shuddered with dread as he tried to comprehend why anyone would have needed to abandon their meal so frantically. As he looked over to the other, entirely unused, placement setting though, his stomach twisted with guilt at the assumption that he had disturbed someone who might have been expecting company.

He laughed to himself at the ridiculous idea that someone could have been waiting for him!

As his gaze fell upon the bottle of wine, he was reminded of his desperate thirst. He could barely contain himself, his hand shaking as he brought the bottle to his lips. The sweet flavour of the wine swirling on his tongue was a welcome relief, even though it wasn't the drink of water that he'd been longing for. Gulping down the wine, his eyes widened with surprise as every drop provided a momentary respite from his dry thirst.

He looked around the dimly lit house, feeling a sense of discomfort. He needed to make a choice, but he wasn't sure what to do. The thought of staying made him feel uneasy, but leaving also seemed less than ideal; if he went back to his car, there would be nowhere else to go so late at night in the middle of nowhere.

With each passing second, the pressure to make a decision grew more urgent.

"Why were you trespassing in my garden?"

With its low and menacing hiss, the feminine voice had taken James by surprise. He snapped to attention, his heart skipping a beat as he registered the woman's presence. Her entrance had been as silent as a whisper. James felt a little sick as her gaze bore into him, waiting for an answer.

He couldn't help but be taken aback by her beauty. She had a fair complexion that contrasted elegantly with her long, flowing locks of dark hair. The cascading length of her dress was the perfect complement to her mysterious aura. With half of her face covered by a translucent veil, James was perplexed as to why she would conceal herself from the world in such a manner. She looked a bit like the woman in the painting, but he thought better of it than to ask.

"Please, forgive me," he urged, his words tumbling out as his throat tightened. "I realise that I'm intruding, but I swear to you, I mean no harm."

The woman seemed to blaze with indignation.

"You should consider the consequences of invading someone's home before you act," she retorted, her voice quiet, but intense.

"I'm sorry," James said, anxious but trying to remain calm. "I've been on the road for days, and when I caught sight of your home, I thought it might be a place for me to rest. I wasn't sure of what to expect, and so I took the risk."

The woman hesitated.

"Oh?" she finally said. "Is that why?"

Before James could answer, a loud roll of thunder made its presence known outside.

"My name's James, by the way," he said, extending an arm for a handshake in the hope that it could lighten the mood.

The woman frowned before stepping back, making it clear to James that she wanted no physical contact.

"It looks like you need a place to stay for the night," she bluntly remarked.

She took a candle in her hand and started walking, leaving James to follow along after her. He found it remarkable to see a woman so beautiful, yet seemingly so isolated in this enormous place. As they strolled down the long corridor, they passed many rooms.

"Rest for the night," she said, pointing to the door ahead of them.

"The house and garden could use some attention," James said, keen to reciprocate his host's kindness. "Do you mind if I lend a hand? I'm experienced – you can trust me to be careful with the work."

He had grown used to having to sell himself.

The woman paused and sighed, her eyes wistful.

"I'll think about it," she murmured before turning to walk away.

The light from the candle she carried gradually declined as she left, cloaking the hallway behind her in darkness.

James surveyed the bedroom, using just the light of the moon to make out shapes and colours. With rain beating down hard on the garden and tapping persistently against the single pane of glass on the window, the storm outside hadn't calmed.

Too tired to decide whether he felt safe in his new environment, James plopped down onto the bed, only for sleep to claim him immediately.

Chapter Two

T he early morning sun shone through the window, already indicating that it was going to be a hot, unforgiving day.

James lay in the unfamiliar bed. With his eyes half-closed, he surveyed his surroundings. He had managed to get some sleep, but his dreams had been upsetting. His mind was still fixed on the nightmares he'd had of a woman desperate in her insanity. He could still recall her terror and unhinged grief as she'd screamed with a haunted wail.

Shaking his head and acknowledging that he'd had a lot on his mind recently, James stretched as he got out of bed and walked towards the window. He was relieved to observe that the morning sky was calm and that the storm had passed. Now that everything had cleared, from his high vantage point, he could see for miles.

Beyond the garden, he spotted a lake. It was coated in a dark green sheen that made it appear deep and still. As much as he yearned to immerse himself in a cooling pool of water, there was nothing about the lake that appealed. Just between the garden and the lake was something that looked like a memorial. With a single headstone at its centre, it was surrounded by smaller stones. There were no flowers or other decorations, making it appear neglected and forgotten. Despite being filled with a restless curiosity and hesitation all at once, James was struck by a profound feeling in his gut, telling him that some places were simply meant to be left alone.

Although the storm had long passed and the grass had only a thin sheen of dew on it, the garden was still shrouded in an air of unease. It caused James to think back to the female shrieks and cries of anguish that had featured so vividly in his nightmares.

Taking a moment to contemplate what lay ahead for him, he reminded himself that being at the house could prove to be a great new opportunity. Motivated to get ready for the day, he moved his hand across the stubble on his face, and decided that he needed to shave.

The bathroom was in a terrible state. The tiles were cracked, and mildew had formed far beyond the corners of the walls. The pipes were rusty, their paint having chipped off long ago, and the sink was filled with debris and cobwebs.

Upon moving closer to the sink, James was startled to see that the small mirror in the cabinet above had been shattered. It reminded him of the shattered glass covering the painting of the exhausted woman. Feeling unsettled, he decided that one more day without a shave wouldn't be a problem.

Not wanting to dwell on the broken mirror, he drew a bath. He was hesitant to spend too much time in the bathroom, but the tub filled quickly with water. He accepted the relief it provided, even though it wasn't the exact temperature that he had been hoping for. He closed his eyes and enjoyed the feeling of the water's crisp chill as it wrapped around him, invigorating his senses and banishing the heat from his body. He didn't mind that the bath hadn't been used in a while and had a slight film of grime on it. He had experienced worse before.

Upon returning to his room, he dried himself off with a towel that he'd found near the sink. As he looked up, his steps faltered when he noticed a neatly-folded dressing gown resting on the bed. It was as though it had come out of nowhere. Feeling uncomfortable, he reasoned that the woman must have heard him in the bathroom and taken the initiative to put the gown out for him. He was, after all, a guest in her home.

He ran his hand along the fabric of the full-length plum-coloured dressing gown. It was plush and soft, feeling so good against his skin. He hadn't experienced something so comforting in a while, and was grateful for the sensation.

He peered out of the window once more, gazing in wonder at his new environment, despite his concerns about it. He noticed that the same raven he'd seen upon setting foot in the house was now perched on a large rock, its glossy feathers iridescent in the sun's rays. Just a couple of metres away, stood the woman. She was watching the raven, a gentle smile on her face, as though she was grateful for the company of her feathered friend.

The raven cocked its head slightly to the side, watching the woman with its black eyes. Suddenly, it stretched out its wings and flew down closer towards her, landing gracefully on the ground. As if performing some kind of ritual, the woman reached out her hand and held it open, and the bird stepped onto her palm.

As much as he was appreciative of the hospitality in his present situation, James reminded himself that he didn't have to stay at the house for any longer than he wanted to.

With the dressing gown wrapped around his athletic body, he made his way downstairs to find a lavish breakfast display set out on the dining table. An array of succulent fruit was laid out on ornate plates, which gave the meal an air of extravagance that seemed far too excessive for a breakfast.

He searched the room for the woman, but she had vanished, as though she didn't want to be in his company. He found it strange that she had seemingly gone out of her way to prepare food for him if she was anxious to avoid him. Too famished to give the situation any more thought, he decided to indulge.

Seating himself at the table, an overwhelming sense of shock and horror washed over him when his eyes fell upon the painting. Its glass covering was no longer broken; what was once fragmented now gleamed with a smooth, pristine sheen.

How could this be? How had someone managed to repair the shattered glass with such speed and precision – all without being noticed? Although the glass looked better for being repaired, there was something about its recovery that simply felt wrong and at odds with all reasonable logic.

James shuddered as he heard the woman's voice from behind him. He glanced over his shoulder to see her standing in the doorway, her presence dominating the entire room.

"That painting has certainly caught your attention," she said. "I have considered your proposal. You may do some tasks around the house, and upon their completion, I will pay you."

James was irritated by her vagueness, but since he had no other prospects, he decided that in the circumstances, it was still an opportunity.

"I see that the glass on the painting has been repaired," he said, fishing for an explanation.

"It looks like it," the woman replied dismissively.

She spoke in riddles and veiled phrases. James knew that any further questions would be met with the same evasive answers, and so, he held his tongue. Her ambiguity was frustrating, but all he could do was grit his teeth and bear it; maybe it was just her way. He had to reluctantly accept that whatever he was going to be paid, it would have to suffice.

Even if he had worked up the nerve to, he couldn't have asked the woman any more questions. With his gaze lingering on the painting, she had already left the room.

Chapter Three

James worked diligently on the house for several days, slowly but surely making progress. It was no easy task; the materials available to him were not the best. The wood often splintered and cracked when he pounded the hammer too hard against it, leaving him feeling helpless. He persevered, steadily repairing and replacing various pieces as he kept in mind that perhaps one day, the house could be unrecognisable from its presently sorry state.

Despite some of his imperfect attempts, James was beginning to make enough progress that he felt he was not wasting his – or his host's – time. As exhaustion caught up with him each night, he took pride in his achievements and looked forward to the day when he could declare the work finished, and of course, receive payment for his labour.

Although he was taken care of, he couldn't deny that the woman's hospitality was rather peculiar. Always, there was food on the table for him, and she would sometimes serve it up and hasten away like a furtive cat. She never joined him whilst he ate, and never gave an explanation as to why.

It wasn't just the dining arrangements though; James found her to be very strange overall. Though he had made several attempts to converse with her prior to sitting down to eat, she had never stayed long enough for a proper conversation. It seemed that, no matter what he said, she would make her way out of the room as soon as possible.

Perhaps she was shy, or simply had somewhere else that she needed to be. James could only assume that, beneath the reticent exterior, was a kind woman. She had, after all, agreed to host him, and had presented him with an opportunity for work.

Very sporadically, the woman seemed to welcome James' presence. Some evenings, she would ask him to join her on a leisurely stroll through the garden. They moved together in a plodding synchronicity, not feeling entirely at ease, yet not feeling wholly uncomfortable either. In those moments, she was rarely talkative, often offering monosyllabic answers, or none at all. She seemed to be trying to contain something, some emotion held tightly within. There was a tension about her, and it was clear to James that she hadn't interacted with anyone for quite some time.

Perhaps she is simply a woman of habit. Perhaps I have disrupted her routine.

One evening, after they had been walking for quite a while, much to James' surprise, the woman reached out to hold his hand. He felt a chill run through his body as her icy fingers entwined in his. Despite the warmth of the summer night, he was shocked by the woman's frigidity and couldn't comprehend how she could feel so cold to the touch. He shuddered, but was too consumed to pull away. He wanted to, but there was something about her contact that startled him to the core.

Upon noticing James' discomfort, the woman seemed immediately offended, which caused her to swiftly move her hand away from him. She then rigidly folded her arms across her slight frame.

Almost angrily, she quickened her pace, and whilst she remained elegant in her movements, she was evidently keen to get back to the house. Out of politeness and not wishing for the tension between them to increase, James had to lengthen his stride in order to keep up with her. With the heavy silence in the air overwhelming, no more words were uttered that night.

Chapter Four

The next few days passed in silence between James and the woman. Every morning, however, he would come down to discover that a freshly-prepared breakfast of fruit and tea had been set out for him. She had a knack for timing; his meal was always ready just as he entered the dining area, yet she herself was always clear of the room.

Every morning when James peered out of the bedroom window, he could see the woman walking in the garden. She appeared to drift around in a dream-like state, her arms limp by her sides, her movement steady and unhurried. It was difficult for him to tell if she was aware that she was being watched; if she was, she did a remarkable job of hiding it. She seemed distant, as though her entire being was somewhere else.

It perplexed him as to why the woman meandered so aimlessly through the garden. She didn't try to cut the weeds or to cultivate the lavender. Her wandering seemed to serve no purpose, but for her, it seemed natural, necessary even. Although something about her curious habit seemed wrong, James had come to be accustomed to it.

Trying desperately to shake off the disconcerting feeling, he attempted to snap his thoughts back to reality. No matter how peculiar the happenings within the house and the garden, and no matter how abnormal the woman's actions, he reminded himself that the end goal was to complete the job and to be out of there in a better financial position than when he had arrived.

"Maybe it's me," he mumbled quietly to himself. "Perhaps I'm the problem, just like how Sherry said I was when she told me it was over."

His mind turned to thoughts of his break-up. It was still stark in his mind, and he hadn't come to accept that the end of the relationship had left him a shell of the man he once was. He had truly believed that Sherry was the one. He had thought they were going to be together forever.

He had always been a bit of a loner, but he had found solace in his relationship with Sherry. They had met at a village dance in their late teens and had been a couple ever since. As the years rolled on, they'd shared so many experiences together. James still couldn't quite imagine a life without her.

Everything had changed. He had come home from a long walk one day to find Sherry sitting on the couch, tears streaming down her face. When she told him that she needed some time alone and that it was over between them, he was devastated.

At first, he'd been unable to eat or sleep, his focus on nothing but his sorrows. He'd been out of work for several months, and it had put a significant strain on their relationship. Sherry wasn't from a tremendously wealthy background, but her expectations were high, and she had a desire for a luxurious lifestyle. James, on the other hand, had been content with a more simple way of living.

For a long time, Sherry had been telling him that she couldn't understand why he wasn't doing more to, as she'd put it, better himself. She would often ask him why he wasn't out looking for work, and would get frustrated when he didn't have a good answer. James had tried to explain to her that he was looking for work, but that it was hard to find something, but still Sherry would accuse him of not trying hard enough.

Their arguments about his unemployment would often escalate, with Sherry saying that he was failing to provide, and that she couldn't stand it anymore. Hurt by her comments, James would then get defensive and remind her that he was doing the best he could.

It wasn't just that though. Even before James was out of work, his relationship with Sherry hadn't been easy. To no avail, they had been trying for a baby, both in the knowledge that neither of them were getting any younger.

In the frustration of the situation, they had found themselves arguing more and more. They would argue about everything – from small things like what to eat for dinner, to bigger issues, to the extent that sometimes, it got too heated, and too personal.

It had got to the point where James felt like he couldn't do anything right. He'd felt constantly guilty, as though he was letting his girlfriend down. He'd known that she was hurting just as much as he was, but it always felt as though she was blaming him for their struggles. He'd tried to talk to her about it, but it would often escalate into another argument.

He had only ever wanted to be supportive and understanding. He had wanted to be there for Sherry, but the more he had tried, the more it felt like she was trying to shut him out.

He'd been confident in his love for Sherry, and in his desire to start a family with her, but it had reached the point where it seemed like it was never going to happen. The thought of losing her had been unbearable, but he hadn't known how to save their relationship.

Deep down, he'd believed that they both loved each other, but the disappointments and pressures of the relationship had evidently come to be too much for them both. He would have been more than willing to work at it. He had even asked Sherry for another chance. However, she'd remained adamant that it was over, making it abundantly, and sometimes cruelly, clear in her explanation.

Ever since he'd said goodbye to Sherry, tears streaming down his face as he'd stood at the door with just a single suitcase of belongings in his hand, James had been on the road. Living off the remainder of his humble savings, he'd had just enough for petrol. For food and warmth, he had hunted and set up makeshift camps in the barren woods all around. By now, he was familiar with the sights, sounds and smells of staying in a new part of the wilderness every night as part of his unfocused travels.

In his present location, he had grown used to the rustle of leaves in the wind outside, and to the occasional draft that found its way through the bedroom. However, he still wasn't quite used to being around the woman, or to the ravens that so often frequented the house and the surrounding garden. He continued to be taken aback every time one of the feathered cohabitants showed up behind him out of the blue.

Chapter Five

T he thought of fixing the roof tiles filled James with dread; of all the jobs that needed doing to improve the house, he suspected that it would be the most demanding. Nevertheless, he couldn't help feeling a little bit of elation at having woken up to the perfect weather for it. Also, he had worked hard to make sure the porch was stable enough to bear the weight of a ladder, and him climbing on it up to the roof.

Letting out a deep sigh, he made sure he had everything he needed for the task. He had no intention of going up or down the ladder any more than absolutely necessary. It had seen better days. The wood was weathered and every rung of its tall length was worn and splintered. In its dilapidated state, it was acceptable for use, but only marginally so.

There was nobody around to ask for help. He couldn't ask the woman. He had a feeling that she would become upset if provoked, and he wasn't keen on finding out what she was like when angry.

He had been having the same nightmare about her night after night. Tossing and turning, sweat dripping off his forehead like raindrops in a storm, he had desperately attempted to escape the vivid depictions of the woman. Her screams were so loud, jolting him to the very core, and her features were always twisted into an expression of unbearable anguish. In every nightmare, no matter how much James had begged his mind to let him flee, all he'd been able to do was watch as the horror unfolded before him.

The intensity of the dreams was such that it felt to James as though the woman was channelling herself directly into his mind. He would bolt awake, convinced she was right there, but every time he leaped out of bed, all he found was emptiness. The sense of dread and loneliness would envelope him like an icy wave, draining away all hope.

Surrounded by only the gentle breeze that softly

swirled its way around the garden in a subtle caress, James carefully ascended the ladder step-by-step, the rungs creaking and groaning with every movement. He promised himself he wouldn't dawdle. He had no desire to linger in the house any longer than necessary, and was particularly eager to finish the roof in a single day.

If it wasn't for the telltale signs of a hole in the roof, he would have considered skipping the job altogether, but, out of respect for the woman, he knew he couldn't ignore the dampness on the interior walls directly beneath the worn parts of the roof. It wouldn't take much to make the wallpaper wet again; just one more storm would do it.

Upon reaching the top of the ladder, James exhaled a sigh of relief. When he closely inspected the most troublesome parts of the roof, the job didn't seem as bad as he had been imagining. He surveyed the area to determine the exact spots that needed his attention, and then placed his repair tools inside the horizontal gutter running along the roof. Filled with hope, he concluded that he could finish before sunset. He knew it wasn't going to be easy, but he was also confident that he had it in him to get the job done. He was up for the challenge.

He smiled to himself, pleased in the knowledge that the work he was about to do would make a significant difference to the woman. It gave him a newfound sense of purpose, despite the discomfort of being up so high upon such a precarious ladder.

His mind and body worked in harmony as he deftly used his hands in a series of precise movements. Applying himself wholeheartedly, his focus and dedication unwavering, he was determined to restore the condition of the roof back to its former glory.

Chapter Six

Squinting against the light of the bright blue sky, James was overwhelmed by confusion. He had no memory of how he had ended up on his back, and the pain radiating from his neck and spine made him hesitant to move. All he knew was that whatever had happened, it must have been beyond his control.

Unable to turn his head, but with his senses heightened, he suddenly noticed that a raven was beside him, the closest any had been since his arrival at the house. He wasn't sure if it was the one that had squawked at him defensively when he'd first set foot inside the building. The bird's feathers lightly touched his arm as it nestled its head into the bend of his elbow. With its glossy black feathers and confident movements, it had an almost ethereal quality to it. James was amazed, yet slightly afraid, uncertain of how to respond. The raven seemed to sense his apprehension.

Still trying to comprehend why the raven had suddenly taken to him, James felt a chill run through his veins as he cautiously shifted his gaze. As his eyes adjusted, he realised he was lying on the grass in front of the house. He tried to recall what had happened, and it gradually dawned on him that he must have taken a nasty fall, although he couldn't remember how or why. Slowly, he jerkily turned his head, and with a sudden surge of pain radiating from his neck, the sight that met him was so startling that a guttural cry of horror tore from his throat.

"You slipped off the roof," said the woman, her voice cold and emotionless.

"When?! How?!" James exclaimed, desperate for an answer.

"We should go inside," she replied tersely as she threw down a wooden cane for him to use.

He reached for her, but it was too late. The woman had already vanished without a trace.

Staring ahead, James gritted his teeth in frustration.

It wouldn't have hurt her to be a bit more accommodating – just this once!

James realised that he would have to move on his own; he wouldn't be given any assistance to rise to his feet, no matter how much he needed it. Apart from the raven, who calmly stood watching him, he was utterly alone with not a soul in sight for miles. Shouting for help would be pointless.

He cautiously crawled onto his stomach and then managed to lift himself up as carefully as possible. His head still spun. He was infuriated at how apathetic the woman was, but she was right; staying outdoors wouldn't benefit him in his current condition.

As black clouds began to gather in the sky, it dawned on James that he must have been unconscious for some time. He turned and struggled towards the house, with the raven trailing behind him.

Chapter Seven

A long, restful sleep did wonders for James. He was able to recall the events leading up to the moment he had ended up on the ground, gazing up at the sky in confusion.

He'd had a dream so realistic he was convinced that it reliably conveyed what had happened. Whilst working on the roof, he had been startled by a loud bang that had caused him to jump. The shift of his weight on the ladder had sent him tumbling. He remembered how in freefall, his stomach had dropped. He recalled the sharp pain he'd felt upon landing. He'd hit the ground hard, winded, and then, there had been nothing but blackness until he'd felt something brushing up against his arm: the raven.

James lay there in bed, paralysed by fear as the sun's rays shone almost mockingly through the window. What had he done to deserve this? Every thought in his head screamed for answers, but all he could do was lay there, helpless and on edge.

He wasn't sure what to do. If he interrogated the woman, he could end up leaving empty-handed after all his labour. Equally though, by continuing to work on the house without bringing up his reservations, he could be putting himself in danger.

He didn't think much of the options before him. He was becoming increasingly disappointed with himself for continually choosing politeness over being more assertive. His habit of kindness had cost him dearly in the past, and he feared it would do the same now with the woman.

Angrily, he clenched his fists. With his emotions ablaze, he hurled his arms up in a desperate plea for mercy before bringing them thundering down on the heaped duvet.

He immediately regretted it when an agonising pain ripped through his back. It served as a stark reminder that he was in no shape to drive away should the woman become impossible. He decided that he would have to be compliant until he was strong enough to leave.

The woman's entrance into the room was so subtle, that in the blink of an eye, she was stood at the foot of the bed.

"My, my," she uttered with only a hint of empathy. "It looks like you ought to relax here until you're feeling better."

"But what about all the jobs I need to finish?"

"That can all wait," she responded quickly before turning to leave the room again.

It perplexed James that the woman didn't appear to be in any hurry to get him out of the house, nor did she appear too concerned that he would be indisposed for a while. He couldn't be sure what she was up to, but he was more certain than ever that it couldn't be anything good.

Chapter Eight

Exhausted from the pain of his injuries, James had easily fallen into a brief slumber. After he awoke, he noticed a bowl full of fruit had been left on the chest at the end of the bed. He assumed the woman had placed it there for him.

"Why did she have to put it so far away?" he muttered, his voice full of irritation.

No matter how hard he tried to ignore the woman's peculiar behaviour, James' thoughts kept returning to it. Yet again his dreams had been filled with noises and visions of her destroying reflectionless mirrors in a fit of despair. Sometimes her face had been so horrifyingly grotesque that he hadn't been able to look away. It would often change to an expression of fury, making her look like a vengeful soul who wouldn't rest until she had punished everyone who had mistreated her.

All frustrations and concerns aside, the bowl of fruit at the foot of the bed looked irresistible. It was an array of colour and freshness, composed of thick-skinned oranges, juicy green apples, and sweet, fragrant plums. Even though it would be a struggle to reach for it, James felt determined. He didn't want to call out for help. He had reached the point where he didn't want to have any further encounters with the woman, convinced that it would be best if he saw less of her.

Cautiously, he attempted to move. At first, he tried to extend his arm to the end of the bed, thinking it would be the least painful endeavour. He soon found out that he was mistaken. A stabbing sensation shot through his lower back. Annoyed, he realised that he would have to get out of bed altogether, and slowly. After exhaling an exasperated sigh, preparing himself mentally, he tentatively twisted his body until his feet were resting firmly on the floor.

He warily stood up, pleased to find that even though his body ached, he was gingerly able to move towards the chest at the foot of the bed. He was glad he had forced himself to get up; it gave him a chance to ascertain whether he was fit enough to make a quick getaway if necessary. A part of him still wanted to leave. However, it was obvious that running would be excruciating; he wouldn't be able to get very far.

I can't even attempt to flee! It would only make the woman angry, and my chances of outrunning her are slim to none.

James grabbed an orange from the bowl and clumsily tugged its peel away, taking in its citrusy scent and admiring the beautiful hues of the fruit. He could feel its smooth surface beneath his fingertips – a sensation that somehow helped him to feel grounded. He closed his eyes and breathed in the sweet aroma. For a brief moment, he felt at peace. He eagerly bit into it, his teeth sinking into its juicy flesh as he welcomed the tart, zesty flavour.

He had barely begun to savour the welcome refreshment when he jumped in surprise.

The woman was standing in the doorway. As she observed him, her face was void of any emotion, yet she stared intently, captivated by each of his movements.

James was so irate that words came out of his mouth before he could stop them.

"What are you doing?! Why do you always sneak up on me like that?!"

Seeming to ignore James' outburst, maintaining her composure, the woman turned away and left, her long dress flowing behind her like a river.

James wasn't sure if he had upset her. Despite his stomach's growls and hunger pangs, and despite how scrumptious the first few bites of the orange had been, he vented his frustrations by pelting it at the floor with such force that it broke up into pieces, juice staining the skirting board nearby.

Too angry to try eating anything else, he collapsed onto the bed and cursed at the jolt of pain that shot right through him. He put his hands to his head and let out a deep sigh. He couldn't figure out what was happening.

Why is she so hospitable and generous one moment, yet so difficult and unyielding the next?

Chapter Nine

James trembled as he perched on the edge of the bed, anxiety coursing through his veins like a raging river. His outburst still ringing in his ears, he feared the worst from the woman he had wronged – yet he was helpless to do anything but await her response. He knew that his actions could not be undone and whatever their consequence, it was something that he would have to face.

He tried to control his racing heart, to restore some semblance of peace in the room, but then, from elsewhere in the house, a thunderous explosion cracked the silence. He now knew that sound – glass shattering from a force delivered with unbridled fury – like the back of his hand.

He waited for the screams that had become so familiar to him in his dreams, but there was only silence.

He rose shakily, and despite the pain still surging through his body, made his way to the bedroom doorway. Again he heard the loud shattering of glass. Against his better judgment, he proceeded to amble down the hallway, desperate to know what was going on.

A feeling of remorse overwhelmed him as he arrived at the doorway of the main lounge, for there stood the woman in the middle of the room. Surrounded by shards of glass, her clothing was dishevelled, but she had no visible injuries. Before James could even register what was happening, she charged towards him, shrieking in a wild frenzy, her face contorted with rage.

Instinctively, James' arm jolted out in front of him, ready to stop the woman, but before his hand could make contact with her, she halted her movement and glared at him, her face twisted in anguish. Her gaze was so intense that he felt as though she was looking into his soul.

He wanted to escape, but he couldn't move. His fear of the mysterious woman kept him rooted to the spot. He was overwhelmed by the danger, and was doubtful as to whether he could talk his way out of it.

"My nightmares are like this," he mumbled, completely baffled. "What is this? What's happening?"

The woman laughed cruelly, seemingly pleased that she had managed to get a reaction. Her lips pressed into a hardened, triumphant smirk. Then, before James could process what was happening, she grabbed the wooden chair next to her and hoisted it up above her head. Incredibly, with her small stature, she managed to keep the chair suspended above her. In that moment, James had no doubt that she was willing to harm him.

"Stop!" he bellowed, his voice reverberating off the walls.

He was not usually one to shout, but he'd had no choice.

The woman immediately set the chair on the floor. As she stepped back from James, a sense of relief seemed to wash over her – she appeared thankful that someone had dared to distract her from her frenzy.

James edged closer to the woman, determined not to back away. He wanted to prove to her that he wasn't scared. He also wanted her to know that she didn't have to be fearful of him. He understood that something terrible must have happened to cause her to become so upset. He felt sorry for her.

The woman retreated to the corner, her expression still flushed with anger. James knew he had to try and diffuse the situation.

"Is this something that happens often?" he asked, immediately regretting how idiotic the question must have sounded to her.

The woman glared at him, her eyes filled with a rage that warned him not to say the wrong thing.

"Do you need me to help tidy up?" he offered.

The woman's expression eased a little. She clearly wasn't worried about the destruction she had caused, but nonetheless, she appeared thankful that someone seemed to care.

James had endured an abundance of female hysteria from many of the women in his life: his mother, his sisters, and his ex-girlfriend. To see a woman vulnerable and in distress wasn't unfamiliar to him.

Of course I want to get paid and get out of here, but a part of me wants to help her. She must be in so much pain.

"It looks as though you've got a knack for destroying glass," he remarked, wanting to know more, but not wishing to come across as invasive.

The woman said nothing in return.

James was desperate to take control of the situation.

"I'm going to get the dustpan and brush," he said. "Stay there. I'll be right back."

***

James' eyes darted around the large cupboard, urgently searching for the dustpan and brush. Setting his gaze upon them, his stomach dropped as he slowly came to a realisation: there was only one thing that needed to be cleaned up – the broken shards of glass that lay strewn across the floor.

Everything else in the room had survived. The woman had destroyed only the glass on the portrait.

But why? he wondered.

***

Tightly grasping the dustpan and brush in his right hand, James took his time walking back to the room. While he was well aware that he could use them defensively if needed, he prayed that he wouldn't have to. It gave him a chill when he thought of the woman's glowering face, her body trembling with hysteria.

His mind turned to thoughts of the numerous ravens he had seen since his arrival at the house. He wished that even just one of them could be present. Having an observer to this madness, even a creature, would have been a comfort to him, just to help him feel that he wasn't going insane.

How could anyone willingly cause so much destruction to their own home?

As he cautiously entered the room, James' heart thundered rapidly. The anticlimax was palpable when he realised that the woman was no longer there.

He had to be sure, and so he searched the room diligently, in case she was hiding somewhere. His anxiety heightening, he even searched inside the cabinet cupboard.

"This is crazy," he muttered.

It irritated him that he had allowed himself to become so consumed by suspicion and paranoia.

I must be losing my mind! There must be a reason for the woman's strange behaviour though. Perhaps it's a cry for help. Whatever it is that's on her mind, she must be severely disturbed by it.

James was positive that he had searched the room thoroughly. Looking elsewhere for the woman would be pointless; with his limited mobility, and with her ability to be so elusive, it would be a futile endeavour.

He made his way to the table he had come to know so well, where he'd enjoyed many breakfasts before things had gone so downhill. As he reached forward to pull out a seat, something caught his eye: a note on one of the placemats. There was no pen or ink anywhere in sight. It was as though the note had just materialised from thin air, and yet, it was clearly intended for him.

The paper was old and tattered, curling up at the edges. James brought it up close to his face, wondering if it had the same musty smell as the house. Sure enough, he could detect an aged odour. He even felt as though his fingers had acquired a coating of dust just by touching it.

He was hesitant to read the note, but he knew that it had to be done:

What I have to say may not be easy to understand, and I'm sorry if it causes you any distress.

I believe there's a reason you've come to me. No matter how complicated things might be, I can't ignore whatever it is that destiny has brought before us.

Please, James, I'm begging you. Please meet me at the far end of the garden. I ache to explain everything to you. Please grant me this.

Yours truly,

Iris

Chapter Ten

James hobbled out of the house onto the wooden porch, and down towards the garden's overgrown pathway. His back ached with each step, but after everything that had happened, he *had* to meet the woman. Going to the far end of the garden to do so, no matter how painful, would be worth it in the name of getting some answers.

He couldn't shake the feeling of unease that had settled in his gut. Trying to steady his thoughts, he inhaled deeply, turning his focus towards the unkempt area around him.

As he made his way deeper into the weeds and overgrowth, he couldn't help but feel as though he was being watched. He glanced over his shoulder, but there was no one there – just the swaying trees and rustling leaves. He shook his head, telling himself it was just his imagination.

Finally, he reached the end of the garden, close to the very spot that he had previously decided to avoid.

The woman emerged from behind a large row of bushes. She looked calmer than she had before: collected, apologetic even. Just as had been the case when they had first engaged, her face was obscured by a veil.

James hesitated a little, a wave of discomfort washing over him. He didn't know what the woman wanted, but he needed to hear her out.

The woman looked up, her face still hidden in shadows.

"I've been waiting for you," she said, her voice low and mysterious.

"Who are you?" James asked, his voice trembling. "You told me your name in the letter. But *who* are you?"

The woman stalled for a moment, then reached up and pulled back her veil. James gasped in shock. Upon calm, close inspection, it was definitely the face of the Iris in the painting. With her expression more relaxed than he had ever seen it before – no longer hysterical, glaring or foreboding – he could see her delicate features clearly. It was the first time he had felt able to properly look at her – *really* look at her. She was a vision of beauty. Her long dark tresses flowed like a river of ink down her porcelain skin. Her eyes, as ethereal as the midnight sky, seemed to hold secrets and mysteries beyond comprehension. Her plush, expressive lips were contorted with concern.

"I'm sorry," she said, her voice full of remorse. "I know I've been incredibly difficult."

James' mind raced as he tried to make sense of what was happening.

"I don't understand," he said, his voice barely above a whisper.

"I don't know if you'll believe what I'm about to tell you," she said. "But please, come with me."

James nodded in agreement. The woman was no less mysterious than she had seemed before, but now, instead of her aura communicating something threatening, there was a focused sense of serenity about her.

"Let's walk," she said.

She moved further into the overgrowth, and James followed along, cautious, but in need of answers.

It was a short walk through the twisted vines and thorny bushes. James soon found himself standing at the very memorial he had spotted from his bedroom window upon his first morning at the house.

He knew he had done right to avoid this part of the garden.

The centrepiece of the memorial was a single weather-worn headstone. Standing tall and overbearing, its inscription had been eroded with time. The smaller stones that surrounded it were nothing more than mere ornaments. There were no flowers, just the moss and lichen growing on the stones that had claimed them as their own over many years.

The air around the memorial was thick with a sense of foreboding. The eerie stillness of the lake nearby only added to the sinister atmosphere. The entire site was a place where even the most outgoing of souls would not dare to tread.

A breeze rustled ominously through the bushes. The branches of the twisted trees creaked and groaned, as if they were mourning the forgotten soul of whoever had been laid to rest here, watching and waiting for someone to remember them. A deep feeling of sorrow lingered, with only the sound of the wind daring to whisper on behalf of the dead.

Upon hearing the distant cry of a bird, James was distracted from his reverie.

The woman beckoned him over to a decrepit stone bench overlooking the headstone and the scene surrounding it. He lingered for a moment, unsure of whether he should approach, but the woman's gentle persuasion was almost hypnotic.

As he sat down, he looked closely at her. Although her face was somewhat obscured by the mist that shrouded her, her eyes held a deep sadness that was impossible to miss.

"You remind me so much of my husband," she said, her voice a soft whisper. "You look a bit like him, and have some similar mannerisms, but you are far more compassionate. Unlike him, you don't beat me, degrade me, or tell me that I'm not worthy. The harshness of his treatment affected me for years. He was always telling me how ugly I am. Even the smallest glimpse of myself in a mirror makes me want to shatter it. Even though my husband passed away long ago, I can't stop myself from lashing out every time. It's a curse that's followed me to the grave."

"The grave?!" James exclaimed. "What do you mean?!"

"James, it pains me to have kept this from you. I need you to understand that I'm not quite like the living. I am, in fact, a spirit, a ghost if you will. It has never been my intention to deceive you, but I didn't know what else to do."

Chapter Eleven

A sick feeling washed over James, draining him to the very core. The information was just too much to take in, too distressing to bear. He had known something was off – he had felt it – but he never could have predicted the truth he now found himself facing.

He took a deep breath, trying to steady himself.

"I tried to keep my distance, really I did," the woman pleaded. "I didn't intend to develop feelings for you. I made an effort to avoid you. In fact, I've gone out of my way to confuse and put you off, but no matter what I do, I can't seem to escape the hand that destiny has dealt."

James wasn't sure what to think. It hadn't crossed his mind before that he could possibly be attracted to the woman – and that was before he'd found out about her being a ghost!

He shuddered again.

"Please don't fear me," she said. "I beg of you. I'll understand if you want to leave, but please, don't fear me."

"I thought you wanted me to fear you?"

"I did. Oh, please believe me that I did. It's just that today in particular, when I caught sight of myself in the painting, I couldn't stand it anymore. All I could think about was how ugly and useless I am."

"I'm sorry you feel that way," James said, sadness lacing his tone.

He still couldn't quite believe that he was talking to a ghost. It felt surreal in how strangely comfortable it was becoming.

"Thank you," said the woman. "It hurts me how even in death, the way my husband made me feel is something that still haunts me."

"Is there anything I can do to help?" James asked, keen to ease the woman's pain.

"Actually, yes, there is," she said. "Will you stay here with me a little longer? I don't even care about the house, or the repairs that need doing. I can manage with everything just as it is. What I really need, to be honest, is some good company. Please, James, will you stay here with me?"

James was now certain that he no longer needed to fear the woman. Instead, he wanted to help her – not only that, but he was intrigued.

"I will stay for a while," he said gently. "I feel that we have a better understanding of each other now. For what it's worth, I'm honoured that you've confided in me. It can't have been easy. Tell me, do you come to this memorial often?"

"No," said the woman. "My husband was laid to rest here, and admittedly, I never could bring myself to tend to his headstone."

"I don't think you're at fault for that," James said. "You've got your reasons."

"Thank you," said the woman. "I'm glad you're going to be staying here with me for a while."

James didn't want to feel responsible for the woman and her situation. He also didn't want her to become too attached to him. However, now that she was no longer a threat, and now that she had confided in him, he felt the need to stay at the house for just a while longer.

"I have to ask," he said, nodding in the direction of the memorial's headstone. "Is your husband a ghost?"

"I doubt it," said the woman. "He was a bully, and was entirely at ease with his foul behaviour. When somebody dies with no remorse, it's much easier for them to cross over to the other side."

"Is that why you're a ghost: because you haven't managed to cross over?"

"I'm afraid so."

"Would you like to cross over?"

"I admit that it would be lovely to finally get some rest," the woman said wistfully.

"Is it too late for you to cross?"

"No," she said. "If the curse of my pained soul could be truly laid to rest, then I could cross over. I must admit, the eternal sleep would be a relief."

"A curse?" James asked. "Can't curses be broken?"

"Yes," said the woman.

"How?"

"With love," she said. "I need to feel love before I can rest for eternity."

Chapter Twelve

James woke up to the sound of birds chirping outside his window. He took a long, satisfying stretch, feeling the warmth of the sun on his face. He smiled, realising that for the first time since he'd arrived at the house, he hadn't had a nightmare. There had been no screams ringing in his ears, and no visions of the woman surrounded by glass in tormented agony.

He sat up in bed and looked around his room. Everything was in its place, and the familiar surroundings were no longer jarring. Still sore from his injuries, he carefully placed his bare feet on the floor and stood up, feeling energised and refreshed; a good night's sleep had made all the difference. He walked over to the window and opened it, letting the fresh morning air fill his lungs.

Confident that it was going to be a better day, he

smiled to himself and got back into bed, keen to embrace his newfound feeling of peace and contentment.

He had already decided what he was going to do.

I'm going to give Iris the love that she was deprived of when she was alive. If that's all it takes to break the curse, if that one thing will allow her soul to go peacefully into the grave, then it will be no trouble at all. I'll give her my very best.

James had already come to accept that whilst he wasn't in love with Iris, he cared about her. He knew that he could give her what she needed. He wouldn't have to pretend. He wouldn't need to feebly humour her. He knew that in treating her well, he could give her the greatest gift of all: the eternal peace that she so desperately longed for.

It's strange to think that if Iris finds peace, she won't be around anymore. I have only ever known this house with her in it.

James rolled over onto his side. Finally able to appreciate the plush mattress and comforting duvet, he could have easily fallen asleep. The musty scent of the room no longer carried with it a threatening sense of unease.

As he happily closed his eyes, he heard a gentle knock on the bedroom door.

"May I come in, please?"

James looked up. It was the first time Iris had approached him gently. She didn't need to creep around or startle him anymore.

"Good morning," he replied. "Come and sit on the bed."

The woman smiled. No longer was there any malice behind her mannerisms. She delicately glided from the doorway to the bed, and elegantly sat down next to James, who had rolled over to be closer to her.

"Thank you for being so honest with me yesterday," he said. "Not only was it brave of you, but I was interested to learn about what you've been through."

He extended his hand towards the woman's. Smiling warmly at her, he made it clear that he wished to share a tender moment.

Although a little shy at first, the woman gratefully laced her fingers into his. Unlike the last time they had briefly held hands and felt jarred by the whole experience, this time, it was perfect.

No longer shocked or confused by the coldness of the woman's touch, James welcomed it, fascinated and endeared not just by the fact that he was connecting with a ghost, but with the woman herself.

"You must have needed to be strong for so long," he told her. "It can't have been easy."

"I always held my tongue when my husband was being cruel with his," she said. "I didn't want him to beat me – not that I could ever stop him anyway."

"He didn't deserve you," James said. "Here, you can settle down next to me if you like. Tell me anything. I'm listening."

The woman looked at him appreciatively, and then delicately settled down next to him. Her every movement seemed to be guided by a subtle calmness that hadn't been present in her before.

James had never seen a ghost in a resting position before, but he was pleasantly surprised at how natural it felt. No longer was the woman tense and defensive, and it radiated throughout her every mannerism.

"Please hold me," she said, her voice a little fragile.

James shuffled his body closer to the woman. Although he was unable to put his arm around her, he made sure that she was fully cradled by him. Yearning to sooth her sorrows, he began to stroke her hair. It felt almost weightless and chalky against his fingers.

"I'm sorry he hurt you," he told her. "I really am. Let me ease your pain."

"Thank you," she said. "That means a lot."

Chapter Thirteen

Without a word, James motioned for the woman to follow him into the main room. He wasn't sure if it would be a surprise for her, but he had moved the furniture around to frame a makeshift dance floor in the centre. Perhaps it was the good night's sleep, or the fact that he no longer felt on edge in the old house, but the pain from his fall was less a source of agony, and more a minor annoyance that would heal soon enough.

Illuminated by several candles that James had lit in advance, the old room still felt eerie, but there was now a warmth to it. Each creak of the wooden floor no longer signified a sense of foreboding, but served as a reminder that, with creativity and engagement, the house could be filled with love and light.

He gestured for the woman to join him in the

centre of the room, and then held out his hand, inviting her to dance with him. Smiling shyly, she humbly accepted. He stood close to her, as if she were solid and real. As he looked into her eyes, he could see the sadness and longing there. She was still not at peace.

Holding her as though she were a delicate porcelain doll, he twirled her around the room with grace and elegance. The woman seemed to float effortlessly in his arms, her ethereal dress trailing behind her in a majestic mist. They glided across the floor, their movements perfectly co-ordinated as if they had danced together for a lifetime. With admiration and empathy, James gazed compassionately at the woman, her expression vulnerable and tender.

The room transformed around them as they danced. The candles flickered, casting an otherworldly glow as shadows seemed to sway along with them. The woman's dress billowed as if blown by an unseen wind. Her hair flowed behind her like a river of onyx. Her form was beginning to seem more solid, as though she was being brought back to life by James' kindness.

Their dance was both melancholic and joyful,

their movements telling a story of love, loss and longing. James whispered sweetly into the woman's ear, telling her that she was worthy and beautiful. He promised to do everything in his power to make her happy; to ease her pain and to help her find peace.

The woman smiled and rested her head on his shoulder, her form becoming more tangible with each step. She seemed to be coming back to life. Similarly, James could feel his own heart filling with hope and joy.

She deserves this. She deserves to be happy, and she deserves to be free.

Chapter Fourteen

The sun was setting, painting the sky a deep orange and pink. James walked arm in arm with the woman. As they moved down one of the garden's cobblestone paths, the only sound was the crunch of his footsteps on the gravel. Neither of them spoke, but a feeling of peace and camaraderie hung in the air. James could sense that the woman felt more at ease than she had in a long time. It was as though the weight of her aura was lighter than it had been before.

As he looked around the garden, taking in the sights and scents around him, James had a new appreciation for it. Nobody was at fault for the state it was in. It had simply fallen prey to the passing of time.

"I bet you took wonderful care of this place when you were able to," he said warmly.

The woman smiled gently, a wave of nostalgia washing over her as she surveyed the now-overgrown plants and weeds.

"Thank you," she said. "I did. I used to spend hours tending to it, making sure every plant was healthy and thriving. I used to enjoy having picnics out here of an evening. On a good summer's night, it was wonderful to see the flowers in full bloom."

"Did your husband join you?"

"No. When he was alive, he would usually go out drinking. It was a relief for me in some ways. It gave me some much-needed time to myself. It was a different story when he came home drunk though."

"Oh," said James, reading between the lines.

"It's ok," said the woman. "When my husband died, the garden continued to give me a lot of comfort and pleasure. It was a place of sanctuary throughout my marriage, and after my husband's passing too."

"Everyone needs sanctuary," James said, thinking back to how when he was with Sherry, he had often yearned for time alone, just to clear his head.

"You can stay here forever, if you like," said the woman.

"Are you sure?" James asked. "Surely the land is owned by somebody?"

"I'm not sure about that," said the woman. "Because I have remained here even in death, I have never thought of this place as being anyone's but mine."

"That's understandable."

"So will you stay here?"

"It would be very different without you here."

"I think so too," said the woman.

"I'm happy to be here enjoying this moment with you," said James, almost too overwhelmed to think so far ahead.

The woman smiled and nodded in agreement. They stood there, arm in arm, watching as the evening rays of light illuminated their surroundings, creating an ambience of tranquillity. The silence between them felt like an embrace; no words were necessary to express their shared understanding.

Their peaceful reverie was soon broken by the cawing of a raven. It landed at the woman's feet. She looked down at it fondly, a gentle smile playing on her lips. Slowly, she bent down and reached out to stroke its back, her fingers brushing against its silky feathers. The raven stood still as she held it in her gaze.

"Your friend has come to say hello," James said playfully.

"Indeed," said the woman. "My ravens have been great company to me over the years."

"Your ravens?"

"Yes," she said. "In death, I was granted the company of nature. I'm lucky that I have always had a couple of ravens willing to stick by me."

"Is that why that raven screamed at me when I first got here?" James asked.

"It is," said the woman, sounding impressed by

James' logic, and amused at the raven's actions. "I feel blessed that they want to protect me. I'm sure they are fine with you now; it's just that nobody ever comes here, and when you turned up, it must have been a shock to them. It was probably natural for them to send you a warning signal. They can be very territorial."

James couldn't deny that the more the woman opened up to him, the more he was starting to enjoy her company.

If only her husband had been good to her. She would have surely thrived with the right support and friendship.

"May we walk to the lake?" he asked. "There's something there that I'd like to show you."

The woman nodded. She seemed cautious of the offer, but not uncomfortable overall.

They walked through the garden in silence, enjoying each other's presence. Eventually, they reached the memorial. With the tall trees and their leaves rustling in the gentle breeze, James led the woman quickly past the headstone and closer to the water.

The lake's surface was undisturbed. James gestured towards it, and the woman stepped closer to get a better look. As she peered into the water, she saw a reflection of herself – a faint outline of a woman with long dark hair, wide eyes, and a small, worried smile. Uncertain, she turned to James for reassurance. He smiled at her, his expression thoughtful, but tender.

"Look back into the lake," he told her. "Tell me what you see."

"That's me," she replied reluctantly.

"Yes, but what do you *see*?"

"I… I don't know," the woman replied, unsure of what James was getting at.

"Let me tell you what *I* see," he said confidently. "I see a beautiful woman – one who is strong and brave; one who has had to carry the burden of someone else's cruelty for far too long. I see a beautiful face, kind eyes, and a smile that could light up any room, given the chance to shine."

The woman looked back at James, her expression one of raw, vulnerable emotion. She had never had anyone be so kind to her before.

"Allow yourself to accept what I'm saying," James insisted. "*Believe* what I'm telling you, and take it to heart."

In response to James' reassuring words, the woman plucked up the courage to turn and look at herself in the lake again; this time, with compassion rather than judgement.

James was moved by the sight. He felt a deep admiration and respect for the woman. He reached out, took her hand in his, and they walked back to the house together in the twilight.

Chapter Fifteen

In bed for the night, James closed his eyes tightly as he willed himself to drift off into a restful slumber. Despite his exhaustion though, sleep eluded him. He tossed and turned, his sheets becoming tangled around his legs as he struggled to find a comfortable position. He sensed that the hour was late.

Just as he thought he would never be able to succumb to the sweet embrace of sleep, a dark and intense dream overtook him. The room around him seemed to fade away, to be replaced by a twisted and terrifying landscape. Unsure of what horrors the dream would reveal, his heart began to race as fear gripped him.

He found himself standing at the edge of an empty grave, the ground freshly turned and the smell of damp earth overwhelming his senses. The texture beneath his feet was soft and spongy, as if everything was still settling from having been disturbed. The empty grave was deep, the sides steep and imposing. The moon shone down on it, casting an eerie glow on the scene. James couldn't help but feel a sense of unease as he looked down, as though the sight before him was a foreboding omen of things to come.

He felt the chill of the night air on his skin. Despite how he pulled his shirt closer to his body in an effort to keep warm, the cold seemed to seep into his bones, settling there like a weight.

Suddenly, he looked down in horror; he could see the ghostly figure of Iris. She was being dragged down into the depths of the grave by a horde of bony withered hands. Emerging from the earth like tangled roots, each one reached out to grab her in a tight grip.

Dressed in a flowing white gown, her hair billowed out behind her as if caught in an unforgiving breeze. Her face was twisted in a silent scream. The sounds jolted around only in James' head, an echo of the woman's fear.

Her eyes wide with terror, the skeletal hands

pulled her further down with force.

The hands were relentless in their determination. Iris struggled against their grasp, her ghostly form writhing and twisting as she tried to break free. The hands were too many and too strong; they pulled her down into the grave with an inexorable force, their fingers elongated and dextrous, their nails violently sharp.

As Iris was pulled further down, James could see the grave growing deeper and darker. The hands seemed to be emerging from the very depths of the earth, as if they were coming from some dark and complex underworld. Iris' face contorted in agony. James could feel her dread and despair as though it were his own.

He felt paralysed, unable to move or look away from the gruesome scene as his heart pounded in his chest. There was a part of him that wanted to reach out and help her, to save her from the fate that awaited her in the depths of the grave, but his body refused to respond. He knew deep down that this was her fate, and that it would be wrong to even attempt to change it.

Deeper and deeper the woman's ghostly form descended into the grave, until she was nothing more than a faint glow in the darkness. James could sense her presence fading, until her very being was nothing more than a whisper on the wind.

In the disturbing silence of the night, the hands had taken Iris into an ether from which there was no return.

Standing at the edge of the grave, staring down into the blackness, James felt a sense of loss and sadness. Despite the sorrow that gripped his heart though, he felt strangely comforted. He couldn't explain why. Perhaps it was because after having been so tormented in life, the woman had finally found the peace she had been denied. He could only imagine the pain and suffering she must have endured in her prime, and he couldn't help but feel that now, in death, she could finally rest, and be free of that torment. The woman's spirit had been set free, finally able to find the peace that had eluded her in life.

With not an emerging hand in sight, the grave was empty. It seemed less ominous now – less a portent of death, and more a symbol of release.

James woke with a start, his pulse racing. As his

eyes flew open, the familiar surroundings of the bedroom provided an immediate sense of relief. He lay there for a moment, trying to shake off the remnants of the dream. He could still feel the chill of the night air on his skin, the scent of the damp earth in his nose, and the echo of the woman's screams ringing in his mind.

He got out of bed and walked to the window, looking out into the night. The moon was still high in the sky, casting a glow on the garden.

Although the dream had been upsetting in some ways, James felt inspired. Besides, it was nothing compared to the dreams he'd had about the woman when he had first arrived at the house; they had been full of a terror and agony that had felt never-ending. His most recent dream, on the other hand, although challenging, had signified to him that one day, perhaps soon, the woman would finally be granted her wish, the curse of her misery broken, and her soul able to fully pass on.

Iris will have the peace that she's been yearning for. I can feel it.

Chapter Sixteen

The next day, James couldn't stop thinking about the dream he'd had. It had felt so real that the images still lingered in his mind. As vivid and as disturbing as it had been though, he was certain of what it meant. He took great comfort in his feeling that the woman would be able to pass on peacefully one day.

Wishing to make the best of his time with her, and keen to give her the love and attention that she so needed, he sat opposite the woman on one of the old chairs in the main room as he nursed a cup of milky tea. Clearing his throat and shifting his weight on the creaking furniture, he caused the woman to look up at him. Her eyes were full of curiosity. He smiled gently at her, taking a sip of his tea before speaking.

"I hope you don't mind," he said. "But may I ask: where were you buried?"

Although the woman didn't seem offended, she clearly hadn't been expecting the question.

"You don't have to tell me," he added quickly, anxious that he had crossed a line. "It's just that one day, I would like to be able to visit your resting place, just to pay my respects, and to place some flowers on your grave."

He saw a brief spark of appreciation in the woman's eyes before she looked away.

"It's ok," she said. "It's just that I hadn't expected you to ask. I'm glad that you have. Nobody has visited my headstone. It stands lonely and unattended – just like my husband's, but in a cemetery rather than in the memorial at the end of the garden."

James decided not to ask why the woman hadn't been buried next to her husband. Whether it was through choice or not, with everything that she'd said about him, it stood to reason that she perhaps wouldn't have wanted to be laid next to him for all eternity.

The woman gracefully stood up. Her steps light, yet with purpose, she moved over to an old wooden display cabinet. Covered in a layer of dust, and chipped with age and a general lack of care, the intricately carved masterpiece had been made with skill. Its ornate embellishments and brass handles worthy of a good polish, it had probably been the pride of the room years ago.

The woman tinkered with some of the items on the shelves of the cabinet. James watched with interest as she studied the various objects that had been messily arranged within various nooks and crannies, each with their own unique purpose and story.

With her hand resting lightly on the brass handle of one of the drawers, she paused for a moment, her fingers tracing the intricate pattern before finally opening the drawer with a soft click. Inside lay an assortment of objects, some useful and some purely decorative. She slowly and methodically began to rummage through them, her fingers caressing each item as if looking for a hidden message.

After a good few minutes, she finally found what she had been searching for – a yellowed piece of paper. She moved confidently back to James, and handed it to him. He nodded appreciatively and began to unfold the square of paper, tracing the irregularities of its aged texture with his fingertips.

"It's a map of the area," she said.

James studied the map, drawing his finger across the faded lines that ran through what appeared to be a village. The colours that had once depicted the unfamiliar area so vividly were now mere muted tones and patches of beige.

There was no date on the map, but as he considered how aged it seemed, it hurt him to think of how long the woman could have been suffering in her lack of eternal peace. He felt an aching sadness rising up within him, but quickly pushed it back down. He knew his emotions could provide no answers, and so, he continued to study the map, following the lines and contours with a practiced eye.

Within the details of the map, he spotted the location of a church, and indeed, a cemetery.

"Is that where you were buried?" he asked, pointing cautiously at the location.

"Yes," the woman said quietly, a lilting melancholy in her tone. "It's quite a way from here. I think it's kind that you're willing to go there just for me."

It hurt James even more to think of how humble the woman could be, and of what must have happened in her life to make her have such a low opinion of herself.

"It would be no trouble at all for me to go and pay my respects," he said with certainty. "I *want* to go and do that. In fact, after everything that's happened, I can't bear the thought of *not* going to do that."

The emotion in the woman's expression was palpable. James' kindness had clearly had a profound impact on her.

He could feel her pain, her sorrow and her gratitude as the intensity of her feelings lingered in the air. In that moment, he was certain that he would never truly know the full scale of everything the woman had suffered – not just in terms of how neglectful her husband had been, but with regards to anything else that she may have been through.

James had never been a man of extremes – his temperament was not one of passionate highs or lows – but he could not ignore the tug of grief that seemed to colour everything about the woman's presence.

He smiled warmly at her, feeling strongly that the least he could do was be there for her in her time of need.

Chapter Seventeen

James awoke at sunrise. The sky was a vivid mixture of sweet peach hues and pale blues, reminding him that even the old house was not devoid of fresh air and nature.

Feeling well-rested, he rubbed the sleep from his eyes. He hadn't dreamed, or tossed and turned, the entire night. He almost felt as though he'd been granted a precious moment of respite from any feelings of fear and uncertainty.

It had been a different kind of sleep to each and every one that he'd experienced since his arrival at the house. There had been no nightmares, no nothing; just pure, restful, undisturbed and comforting sleep.

As he enjoyed the feeling of tranquillity all around him, and the comfort of the soft duvet covering his body, he couldn't help but notice a sensation of emptiness in the air. It was as though the house was devoid of any presence other than his own.

Could this be? Could this really be? Could Iris finally be at peace?

James had never been the most intuitive of people. It was something that he had often blamed for the failure of his relationship with Sherry. On this occasion though, there was an overriding feeling in his gut that he simply couldn't ignore, and deep down, he just knew that he had to trust it.

It just feels as though Iris isn't here anymore.

He didn't want to call out for her. He reasoned that he didn't want to alarm her or disturb her from whatever kind of eternal rest that she may now have succumbed to.

He hadn't expected to feel a sense of loss at her passing on, but nevertheless, the feeling was impossible to deny. It was overwhelming and very much at the front of his mind, even if they had got off on the wrong foot when he'd first arrived at the house.

He was confident that he'd done the right thing. He knew Iris had been suffering tremendously, trapped within the walls of the ancient house, and with no respite from her racing thoughts. In having chosen to treat her with the love and care that she had so desperately needed, he knew that he'd given her what nobody else could have: the freedom of eternal rest.

Still though, as he rolled over in bed and gazed out of the window into the subtlety of the morning light, he felt a sense of loss like nothing he'd ever experienced before. Little had he realised it at the time, but he had been enjoying getting to know Iris; he had appreciated her company and grown to welcome their conversations, and their walks around the garden. There was a part of him that even felt honoured that she had confided in him. James hadn't been particularly close to many people in his life, but with hindsight, it dawned on him that being in Iris' company had been a source of comfort.

He swung his legs out of bed and shuffled across the creaky floorboards, drawn towards the door of the bedroom. The house felt so different now. There was a stillness in the air that made the atmosphere feel entirely different, and a silence that seemed to echo with the absence of his ghostly companion.

As he stepped into the darkened hallway, he was struck by the sense that he was now truly alone. He couldn't feel any kind of presence – neither tormented nor content. All around him, a sense of peace seemed to radiate from every corner of the house. He knew, without a doubt, that Iris was now at rest, and deservedly so, free from the pain and suffering that had haunted her and every crevice of the old house for so long.

James walked slowly through the silent halls, his footsteps echoing strangely in the serenity of it all. Although he felt sad for how much he would miss Iris, it was mixed with a peculiar sense of liberation. He knew that his friend was no longer bound to the earthly plane, and was now free to move on to whatever it was that awaited her in the great beyond.

Lost in thought, he sat down in a high-backed chair in the main room. He knew that the house would never be the same again. Aware of the intensity of everything he'd experienced, he allowed himself to sit in silence. The time that passed could have been minutes, or perhaps even hours. It didn't matter. James knew that what he'd been through was not to be underestimated and he wanted to allow himself a moment to process it all.

Eventually, he stood up and walked across the dusty floor, past the table that he had dined upon so many times, and past the painting that he had seen upon first entering the house. The glass was intact. Once Iris had confided in him, no longer had she charged at it in a violent flurry of self-hatred. There was a part of James that wished he could take the painting with him, just as something to remember Iris by. He knew it wouldn't be right to remove it from the wall though – not after it had been there for so long. He reasoned that the house should be left to stand as a monument to Iris, and that even if sometime in the future, somebody else should choose to intervene with the land and everything upon it, he wanted nothing to do with such invasion. He had already decided that now Iris was finally at peace, he would leave the house for good and hold every memory of it only in his mind.

He looked out of the window, gazing out at the precious garden that Iris had made so much her own. He knew that life would go on. It had to. He couldn't dwell on the past. Seeing what it had done to Iris had taught him that.

As he paced around the house, planning what he was going to do next, no longer was there the faintness of a dusty shimmer in the air. No longer did he feel the need to rub his eyes and check that he hadn't been fooled by a trick of the light. No longer did he sense that any moment now, the surprise of seeing a ghostly glow – or a shadow in a doorway – was about to divert his attention. No longer was he on edge or in anticipation of what to expect next. No longer did his heart beat a little faster in expectation of witnessing the outline of a figure, hazy and translucent, but unmistakably there.

"Goodbye, Iris," he whispered, perhaps more to himself than to the woman.

The feeling of closure was enormous. It was more than closure though. James had grown to care very deeply about Iris. If he was being honest with himself, he had probably grown to love her somewhat too.

He promised himself that upon leaving the house, he would do everything possible to make the best of his life: to love and appreciate himself, his needs, and his dreams. No longer would he yearn for Sherry, or grieve their relationship, which had so evidently ended for good.

He was going to appreciate every day. He didn't quite know exactly what that would look like yet. Besides, there was something of tremendous importance that, after leaving the house, he needed to do first.

Chapter Eighteen

It had taken James a while to get to the village, but he was grateful that his car had been up to the job. As it had chugged down the winding country roads, taking him miles away from the old house, he had journeyed onwards with certainty, with no doubt in his mind, and almost with a sense of duty.

Even when the dusty roads had crossroads branching off towards other directions, he had known which route to take. Prior to setting off, he had memorised the map with dedication, determined to get it right for Iris.

His old car had bumped and jostled along the way, and with the many trees looming overhead from the abundance of woodland and ancient overgrowth, the distance between the old house and the village was not lost on James as he'd put his foot down on the accelerator.

It made him a little sad to think of how far away from the old house Iris had been buried. She had, after all, dwelled there for so long in her ghostly form.

Maybe it's for the best, he thought. *At least she's miles away from her husband, and indeed, probably from some incredibly painful memories.*

Setting out on his walk through the old-fashioned village, James saw how the cobblestone streets were lined with charming cottages, each with their own unique gardens filled with colourful flowers.

Iris would have loved this.

As he strolled, he couldn't help but succumb to a feeling of nostalgia. The village seemed to be frozen in time. It had only tall, black ornate lampposts and barely more than a couple of cars in sight.

He passed a small bakery, the sweet aroma of freshly baked bread and pastries wafting out through the open windows.

Yes, Iris could have happily lived here, with a

man capable of giving her the love, care and compassion she so deserved.

James decided to pop into the bakery and treat himself to a delicious pastry. He didn't feel much like eating, but he had already skipped breakfast; now felt like just as good a time as any to replenish his energy.

With the sugared treat in his hand, he sat on a bench just outside the bakery. He couldn't help but notice the friendly locals as they went about their day. Everyone seemed to know each other, exchanging greetings with warm smiles and cheerful waves. It was in stark contrast to what the last few weeks had been like for James. Even when he had been enjoying his time with Iris, every moment spent at the old house had been somewhat isolating overall.

Wiping the pastry crumbs from around his mouth, he thought back to the map and continued walking in the direction of the cemetery.

Still not quite ready to face the memorial that he hadn't been able to stop thinking about, he paused at a picturesque pond. He gazed down at his reflection in the crystal-clear water. There were quite a few frogs swimming lazily within the plant life beneath the surface. He sighed and sat down on the grassy bank, watching as children played and laughed nearby.

It comforted him to think of how Iris' final place of rest seemed so full of life, gentle and constant, with joyous activity all around. The idyllic village wasn't a particularly exceptional or special place, but still it exuded a welcoming, tranquil, and reassuring energy. James hated the thought of Iris being anywhere else. As much as the old house had been her home, it still held painful memories; he felt it wasn't good enough for her.

He exhaled heavily as he stood up, grateful that Iris had finally passed on, but with a feeling of great sadness washing over him as he prepared to pay his respects at her final resting place.

The path leading towards the cemetery was peaceful, surrounded by tall trees and lush greenery. The leaves rustled gently in the breeze, creating a symphony of echoes that was both soothing and eerie at the same time. The sun's rays cast shadows over the landscape, giving everything an otherworldly appearance.

As James continued to walk, he couldn't help but notice the feeling of anxiety building in the pit of his stomach. He was on unfamiliar territory, and wasn't quite sure what to expect. His experiences over the last few weeks had taught him to be wary of those who walked the earth not as the living, but as lost souls – desperate, taunted and afraid. He tried to push the thoughts from his mind, diverting his focus back to the beauty of the surrounding village.

Further on, the path began to narrow, the trees standing closer together. Just a little way ahead, it opened up into a clearing, and James found himself stood at the entrance to the cemetery.

Some of it looked modern, whilst other parts looked several hundred years old. Some of the headstones were made of white marble and had been lavished with an abundance of flowers, gifts and trinkets, whilst others – especially towards the back – were overgrown with moss and weeds.

As James walked respectfully among the headstones, he took his time to read some of the names and dates etched into them. Some dated back to a few centuries ago, whilst others were more recent.

Standing at the back of the cemetery to get his bearings, James looked around, and, having decided how to proceed, began walking towards a headstone at the furthest corner. Based on what Iris had told him about the circumstances surrounding her burial, it made sense to him to take a systematic approach; with no friends or family around after her husband had so cruelly alienated her from those who she had been close to before her marriage, Iris' funeral had been strictly functional, and the approach to her burial had been carried out in much the same manner.

After studying the numerous headstones at the back of the cemetery, by process of elimination, James stood before what he believed to be Iris' place of rest. Nobody had visited the headstone in what seemed like an eternity. It appeared to be one of the few that had been left unattended. Forgotten and neglected, it was without flowers, and without offerings of any kind. Even the groundskeeper had deserted it.

As the years had rolled along, nobody had come to pay their respects; the headstone's name inscription had been slowly eroded by the elements, leaving behind a strange blankness, as if the woman had never existed.

As he slowly traced his hand along the worn engraving, James could confidently feel the letters.

"Iris Dalton," he said softly. "I hope you're at peace now."

He couldn't help but feel an intense sorrow for the woman, as though her existence had been nothing more than a whisper on the wind. For him though, her story had become a part of his own; *he* would never forget her.

James promised himself that he would keep an eye on the forgotten headstone. It was the least he could do after everything the woman had shared with him.

Having brought a single white rose with him to signify love, purity, and peace, he placed it tenderly upon the sodden ground. Reflecting on the vulnerable beauty of the woman's soul, he stood stoically in a reverent silence as the sun slowly sank below the horizon. Only when the last ray of light had disappeared did he consider leaving.

The light breeze of the evening seemed to caress him, offering a comfort beyond words. As he turned to walk back through the cemetery, a single tear rolled down his cheek.

* 9 7 8 1 9 1 3 7 7 9 9 4 8 *